For Tim, who believed I could do it, and Emily, who got me started — N.Y.D.
To Ian, with love — B.T.

Author's Note

Traditional Malaysian tales have always been handed down from one generation to the next, and this was one of many that my mother told me when I was a child. Because I was unable to find it in a book when I grew up, I decided to write it down so that it would not be forgotten.

Many Malaysian stories give human personalities to familiar animals. The tiny mouse deer found throughout Southeast Asia, who outwits larger and more dangerous animals, is in many of them, often as a hero. Adele de Leeuw writes in *Indonesian Fairy Tales*, published by Frederick Muller Limited in 1966, that, because of its small size and alert nature, the mouse deer is held in great affection, particularly by children, who identify with its ability to outsmart larger creatures.

SIMON & SCHUSTER BOOKS FOR YOUNG READERS
An imprint of Simon & Schuster Children's Publishing Division
1230 Avenue of the Americas, New York, New York 10020
Text copyright © 1996 by Noreha Yussof Day
Illustrations copyright © 1996 by Britta Teckentrup
Originally published in Great Britain by ABC, All Books for Children,
a division of The All Children's Company Ltd.
First American Edition, 1996.
SIMON & SCHUSTER BOOKS FOR YOUNG READERS is a trademark of
Simon & Schuster.
Book design by Anna-Louise Billson
The text for this book is set in Quorum
The illustrations are rendered in cut paper
Printed and bound in Hong Kong by South China Printing Co. (1988) Ltd.
10 9 8 7 6 5 4 3 2 1

Library of Congress Cataloging-in-Publication Data
Day, Noreha Yussof.
Kancil and the crocodiles / by Noreha Yussof Day ; illustrated by Britta
Teckentrup. — 1st American ed.
p.   cm.
Summary: A mouse deer and a tortoise trick some hungry crocodiles into
helping them cross a river but fail to plan for their getting back.
ISBN 0-689-80954-9 (hardcover)
[1. Folklore—Malaysia.] I. Teckentrup, Britta, ill. II. Title.
PZ.1.D3216Kan 1996
398.2'09595'045—dc20
[E] 95-50526

KANCIL
and the
CROCODILES

A TALE FROM MALAYSIA

written by
NOREHA YUSSOF DAY

illustrated by
BRITTA TECKENTRUP

SIMON & SCHUSTER
BOOKS FOR YOUNG READERS

Once upon a time, there was a
tropical forest full of parrots, orangutans,
monkeys, and crocodiles, all of whom
could talk.

The parrots talked to the orangutans,
the orangutans talked to the monkeys,
the monkeys talked to the crocodiles,
and the crocodiles talked to anyone who
would listen. All the animals lived happily
together, as long as they were careful to
talk to the crocodiles—who were always
hungry—from a distance. Rare arguments
were settled by the king.

Kancil, the mouse deer, and Kura-Kura, the tortoise, also lived in this forest, and they were the best of friends.

One hot, sunny afternoon, they were walking along the river. Kancil was thirsty. "Wouldn't it be nice to eat some juicy fruit now?" he asked.

Kura-Kura agreed. They walked farther, and passed a few lazy crocodiles floating in the river. "Hello!" called one.

"Hello, Buaya!" answered Kancil. He was always friendly to the crocodiles, because he didn't want to become their lunch.

Suddenly, Kancil saw a rambutan tree on the other side of the river. It was full of ripe, juicy fruit. "Kura-Kura! Look! Rambutans!"

"Oh!" said Kura-Kura. "But how are we going to get them?" he asked, looking at the crocodiles.

Kancil was quiet. Kura-Kura was also quiet. He knew that Kancil was thinking. Then Kancil exclaimed, "Ah!" And he whispered to his friend.

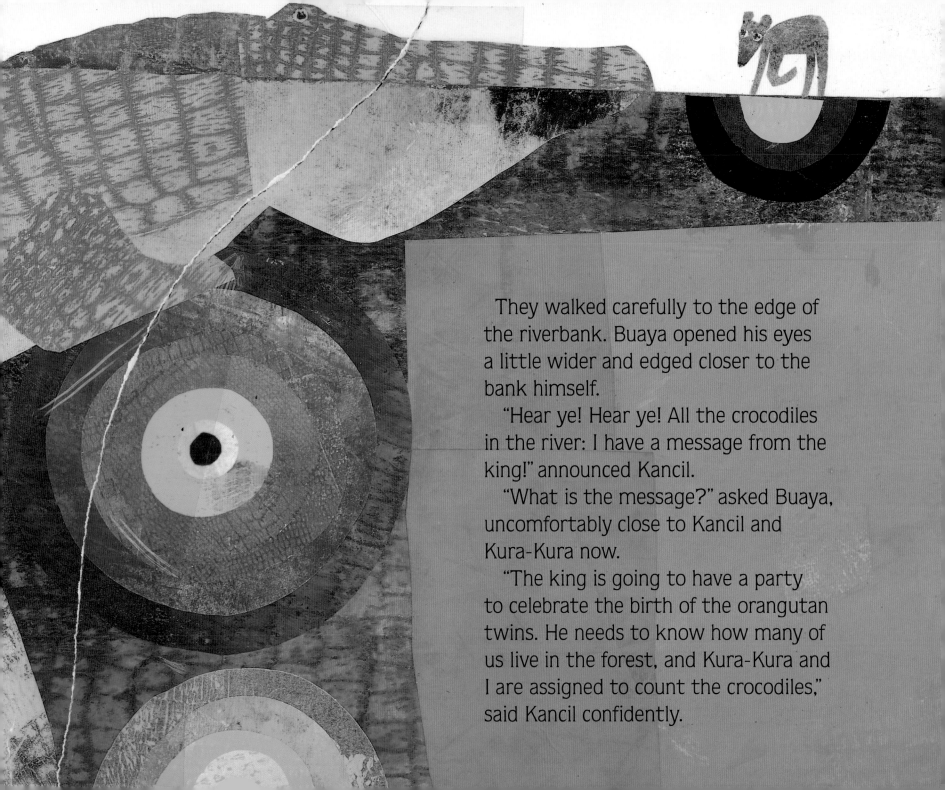

They walked carefully to the edge of the riverbank. Buaya opened his eyes a little wider and edged closer to the bank himself.

"Hear ye! Hear ye! All the crocodiles in the river: I have a message from the king!" announced Kancil.

"What is the message?" asked Buaya, uncomfortably close to Kancil and Kura-Kura now.

"The king is going to have a party to celebrate the birth of the orangutan twins. He needs to know how many of us live in the forest, and Kura-Kura and I are assigned to count the crocodiles," said Kancil confidently.

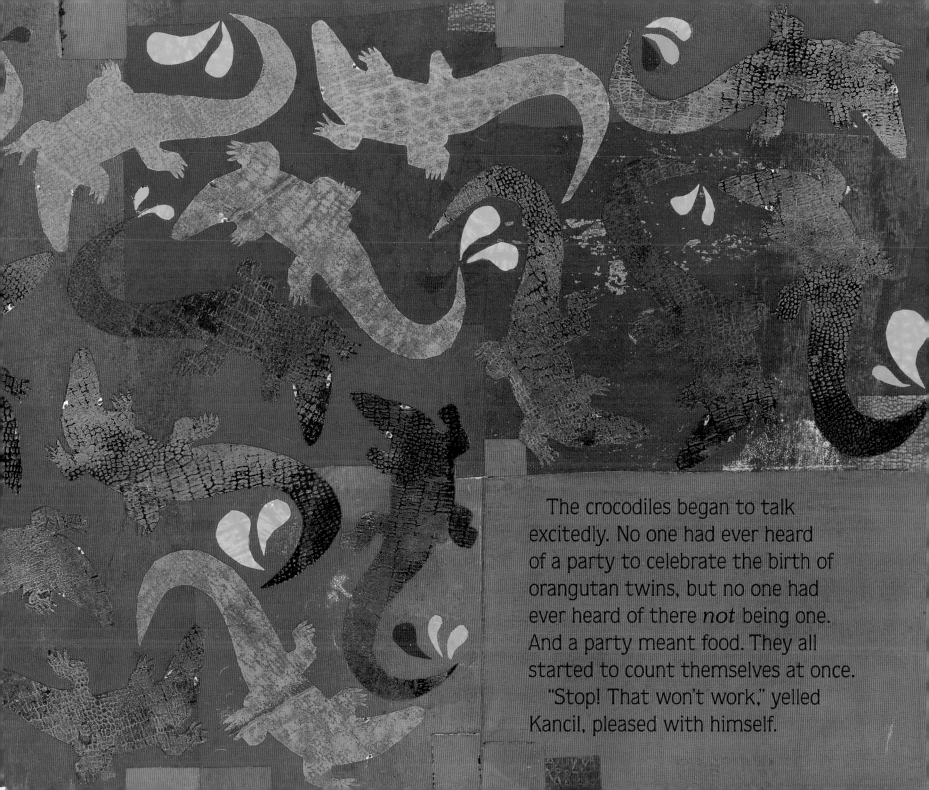

The crocodiles began to talk excitedly. No one had ever heard of a party to celebrate the birth of orangutan twins, but no one had ever heard of there *not* being one. And a party meant food. They all started to count themselves at once.

"Stop! That won't work," yelled Kancil, pleased with himself.

"What do you suggest, Kancil?" asked Buaya.

"Well. If you all make a straight line from here to the other side of the river, we can walk along and count."

"Yes! A good idea," agreed the crocodiles, all pushing to be first.

"Stop pushing!" commanded Buaya.
And all the crocodiles formed a neat line
and tried to stay still.

"Be careful, Kura-Kura," Kancil whispered.
"They won't be interested in us while they
think about the party. Count loudly."

And he stepped out onto Buaya
and called out, "One crocodile!"
Kura-Kura followed behind and
repeated, "One crocodile."
Kancil moved forward and
continued, "Two crocodiles!"
Kura-Kura echoed,
"Two crocodiles."
And on they went.

Finally, they reached the other side.
The crocodiles swam close to the bank.
Buaya sidled up and asked, "How
many of us are there?" He had
been too far away to hear.

"There are twenty-seven greedy crocodiles, Buaya," said Kancil proudly.

"What do you mean?" asked Buaya, upset at being called greedy.

"There is no party. We just wanted to cross the river to get these rambutans. Thank you for helping us," Kancil said.

"We won't forget," added Kura-Kura politely.

"We won't forget, either!" cried Buaya furiously as all the crocodiles grumbled and snapped.

But Kancil and Kura-Kura were already walking toward the rambutan tree with its red, juicy fruit hanging on every branch.

"There is one thing I didn't think of, though," Kancil told his friend. "How are we going to get back?"